CW01066958

£1.00

Christopher

by Regine Schindler
Illustrated by Eleonore Schmid

 St Paul Publications

A long, long time ago, in a land far away to the east, there lived a man who was twice as big as an ordinary man. He was very strong, but his face scared everyone. "Look at that dog-face!" said some. "Ugh, he has a big mouth like an animal," said others. Lots of people would shout "Man-eater!" after him.

The man's name was Reprobus. It means "The Damned".

Big Reprobus left the land where he was born.

"I am so strong," he said, "that I want to serve only the most powerful king in all the world."

He looked for the most powerful king in all the world and he thought, "Maybe this king can rid me of my horrible face. I would like to be a proper human being. I would like to stop being called 'The Damned' and scaring everybody."

Reprobus soon found a king with a large palace and lots of servants. "He is the most powerful king in all the world," the farmers on the roadside told him. They pointed at the high towers of the king's palace.

This king made good use of Reprobus. He made him his chief servant. Reprobus was strong. He could tear up trees with his hands. He could carry five big poles at once. He was tall. He could put roofs on houses without even needing a ladder. He was bigger than everyone else. The king was very pleased about that.

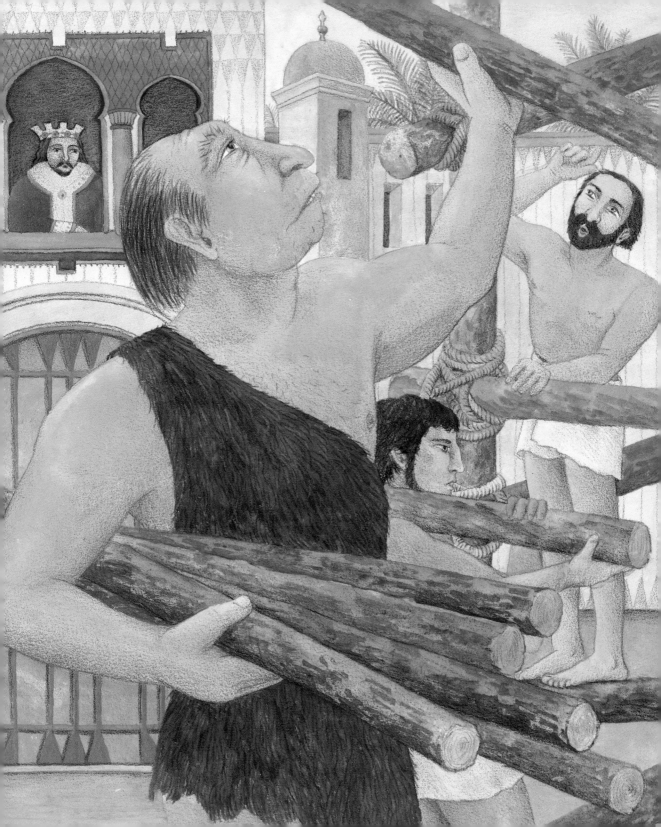

One day a story-teller came to the court of the most powerful king in all the world. Everyone listened to him. But whenever the word "Devil" was said the king would jump. As quick as he could, he made the sign of the cross on his chest.

Reprobus was surprised. He asked the king about it. He asked again and again. Finally the king owned up:

"I am scared of the Devil. I want to protect myself with the sign of the cross."

"Scared?" said Reprobus. "Is the Devil more powerful than you? Must you fear him?"

The king nodded. Then Reprobus turned his back on the most powerful king in all the world and said, "I will look for the Devil. He is more powerful than you. I want to serve him. Maybe he can help me better than you."

For Reprobus had still not lost his dog-face. "I would like to be a proper human being," he said. How he longed for it!

He took only one horse from the king's stable and rode out into the world again.

A troop of horsemen came up to him in a desert. They wore expensive armour that flashed like fire in the sun. In the middle of them rode one whose armour shone like pure gold. The golden rider had a terrifying face. His eyes glowed like hot coals. He galloped up to Reprobus and asked, "Who are you looking for?"

"I am looking for the Devil. I would like to serve him," said Reprobus.

"I am the one you are looking for. I can make use of you," said the terrifying rider.

Soon Reprobus was the Devil's chief servant. He was given a suit of armour the colour of flame. It was covered with precious jewels. Because he was so big and strong, Reprobus was often able to help the Devil. He could throw a spear that was twice the size and twice the weight of any other spear. He rode as fast as his new master, and went with him throughout the world.

But Reprobus noticed that whenever the Devil saw a cross in the distance, he would leave the road. He would ride through the rocky desert, meet dangerous wild animals, struggle through swamps. Only when he was a long way away from the cross would he go back to the road.

The Devil trembled so much then and was so weak that Reprobus had to hold him up.

Reprobus was surprised. He asked the Devil why. He asked again and again. Finally the Devil owned up:

"I am scared of the cross. It reminds me of someone. He was nailed to the cross and killed. He was called Christ."

"Scared?" said Reprobus. "Is this Christ more powerful than you? Must you fear him?"

The Devil nodded. Then Reprobus turned his back on the Devil and said, "I will look for this Christ. He is more powerful than you. Maybe he can help me better than you."

For Reprobus had still not lost his dog-face. "I would like to be a proper human being," he said. How he longed for it!

He threw down his flame-coloured armour full of jewels at the Devil's feet. The only thing he took with him was his spear that was twice the size of any other spear. He rode away to look for Christ.

Reprobus rode across the world for years and years and years. Everywhere he went, he asked about Christ. "A powerful king by the name of Christ? No, we have never heard of him," was the only answer he got.

Then one day he came to the little hut of a hermit. He went inside. In it there was a small wooden cross.

"Do you by any chance know Christ?" he asked. "I would like to serve him."

The hermit told him about Jesus – about his birth in a stable, about his miracles, about his preaching, and about his death on the cross.

"How can I serve a dead man?" asked Reprobus. "I don't understand."

"He is not dead," said the hermit. "He rose again and is alive. If you fast and pray, Reprobus, you will become his servant."

This made Reprobus sad. "I can't do that," he said. "If I fast I will lose all my strength, and I've never learned to pray."

The hermit thought a while. Then he said, "Do you see that big river down there? It flows very swiftly and is full of whirlpools. People are often drowned when trying to cross it." Reprobus listened. The hermit went on, "You are bigger and stronger than anyone I know. Why don't you stand in the river and carry all the travellers across? In this way you too can serve Christ. But be patient. Maybe you will see him one day." "I will take your advice," said Reprobus.

He built himself a little house by the river. Leaning on his spear that was twice the size of any other spear, he carried people across the dangerous river: young and old, rich and poor, kings and beggars. He did this for many years. Sometimes he was tired and sad. In the water he could always see his face looking back at him – his dog-face.

More and more people came and went. But his ugly face stayed the same.

One day while Reprobus was resting in his little house, he heard a child's voice calling.

"Come out and carry me across," it said.

Reprobus went out, but he could not see anyone.

The voice called a second time. Again he went out and again nobody was there.

After the third call, however, Reprobus found a little child sitting on the river bank.

He lifted the child onto his shoulder and stepped into the swirling water. But the waters grew swifter and higher, and the whirlpools became even stronger, and the child on his shoulder seemed heavier and heavier – heavier than all the king's poles, heavier than the Devil in his golden armour, heavier than lead. Then his spear broke in two as he leant on it. The man thought he was certain to drown and the child with him.

But with his last ounce of strength he reached the other bank.

When the strong man had set the child down, he fell tired out to the ground. He said, "Child, I almost drowned with you. You are heavier than the most powerful king, heavier than the Devil. I believe you are as heavy as the whole world."

And the little child ran his hand over the dog-face and through its untidy hair, and answered, "Yes. But you carried more than the world. You carried God who made the world and everything in it. For I am Christ, your God and your king. You have been my good servant and will go on serving me for the rest of your life. Because you carried me on your shoulder you are no longer Reprobus, 'The Damned'. You shall be called Christopher, which means Christ-bearer, a person who carries Christ. From now on you will carry me in your heart and tell the whole world about me. To show that I speak the truth, stick your spear in the ground near your house and see what it turns into."

With that the child disappeared.

The strong man waded across the river back to his little house. But on the way he noticed his face in the water. The dog-face had gone and his big mouth too. A bearded man gazed back at him.

"Christopher, Christ-bearer," he said to himself. "Christ has made a proper man of me. I no longer have a dog-face."

After that he stuck his spear in the ground and went into his house. He lay down, happy and very, very tired.

The next day there was a wonderful tree growing next to the little house. It had leaves, blossom and fruit all at once.

Then Christopher went out into the world. He told people about Christ, "He is the most powerful king in all the world. You may not see him. But he is with you!"

And he told people about himself:

"Once I had a face like a dog, but Christ made a proper man of me."

Notes for parents and teachers

The first evidence for the veneration of St Christopher dates from the fifth century, when a church was dedicated to him in Chalcedon on the Bosporus. He lived in the third century in Asia Minor and died a martyr. In the sixth century a chapel was apparently dedicated to him in Reims, France, and by ca. 600 his cult appears to have reached Spain. Around the year 1000 his name was frequently mentioned in Constantinople, and at about the same period, in what is now called Switzerland, the hospice at Pfafers on the main north-south route was dedicated to him. In the late Middle Ages his intercession was sought more frequently and is found in various prayers for use at Mass. And after the Second World War the veneration of Christopher, the traveller's friend, became very popular. But in 1969 he was deleted from the Catholic calendar of saints.

Naturally these few dates for the cult of St Christopher are meaningless without the legend that lies behind them, a legend with fairy-tale characteristics repeated in many different forms around the Mediterranean. In stark contrast to Martin of Tours, there is no historical "Vita", no biography of Christopher. But there are, apart from the legends, many pictures and images of him.

Luther called Christopher "the epitome of the Christian". As such he is an appropriate figure also for children to identify with... Christopher is a giant. In Eastern versions of the story he has the head of a dog. He was called Reprobus, meaning the "reprobate", "damned", or "despicable". But by his baptism, through meeting Christ, he lays aside his animal being. Becoming a Christian means becoming a "proper" human being. Nevertheless, a long and difficult journey is needed to achieve this, and it involves a continual searching and starting again. Time and again Reprobus wants to find the world's most powerful ruler and serve him. His repeated setting out anew, his overcoming of dangers, and also his readiness to serve are the fairy-tale motifs which give the story its vividness. Furthermore, the fact that help comes from the weak, first in the form of a hermit and then in the form of the little, helpless Christ-child, serves to show how God acts in our lives. This Christ is poor, weak, a real human being, yet also the king of the whole world, strong, a helper in time of need. The miraculous tree at the end of the story stands for this abundance.

This little book is written with the hope that, by means of the legend of St Christopher, children may experience something of the paradoxes and the contrasts that it contains and make them part of their own lives. This should happen mostly through following the story intently and looking at the highly evocative pictures. The meaning of the tale can then enter deeply into the child's unconscious mind. A conscious application of the story to life, a directed discussion, should not really be necessary.

Original title: *Christophorus* © 1985 by Verlag Ernst Kaufmann, Lahr
Translated from the German and adapted for English by Anne Richards and Callan Slipper

St Paul Publications
Middlegreen, Slough SL3 6BT, England
English translation copyright © St Paul Publications 1990
ISBN 085439 306 4
Printed in West Germany

St Paul Publications is an activity of the priests and brothers of the Society of St Paul and
the Daughters of St Paul who proclaim the Gospel through the media of social communication